The New Adventures of

MARY-KATE & ASHLEY ™

The Case Of The

FLAPPER 'NAPPER

Look for more great books in

series:

The Case Of The Great Elephant Escape
The Case Of The Summer Camp Caper
The Case Of The Surfing Secret
The Case Of The Green Ghost
The Case Of The Big Scare Mountain Mystery
The Case Of The Slam Dunk Mystery
The Case Of The Rock Star's Secret
The Case Of The Cheerleading Camp Mystery
The Case Of The Flying Phantom
The Case Of The Creepy Castle
The Case Of The Golden Slipper
The Case Of The Flapper 'Napper

and coming soon
The Case Of The High Seas Secret

The New Adventures of
MARY-KATE & ASHLEY™

The Case Of The

FLAPPER 'NAPPER

by Judy Katschke

HarperEntertainment
An Imprint of HarperCollins*Publishers*

A PARACHUTE PRESS BOOK

PARACHUTE PRESS

Parachute Publishing, L.L.C.
156 Fifth Avenue
New York, NY 10010

DUALSTAR PUBLICATIONS

Dualstar Publications
c/o Thorne and Company
A Professional Law Corporation
1801 Century Park East
Los Angeles, CA 90067

HarperEntertainment

An Imprint of HarperCollins*Publishers*
10 East 53rd Street, New York, NY 10022

THE CAT'S MEOW

"Now *this* is what I call riding in style!" I told my twin sister, Ashley. I leaned against the backseat of the fancy white car.

"Tell me about it." Ashley grinned. We had been inside big cars before—but nothing as serious as a 1920s-style Rolls Royce!

Our basset hound, Clue, stretched out across our laps. "Clue seems to like it, too," I said. "She hasn't stopped drooling since we got into the car."

"Don't remind me!" our friend Patty

O'Leary complained. "This car is fit for a princess—not a dog!"

That made Ashley and me giggle. Patty doesn't know it, but we call her "Princess Patty." That's because she acts a little spoiled sometimes.

"Besides," Patty went on, "Great-grand-mother doesn't even *like* dogs."

The three of us were going to visit Patty's great-grandmother, Fiona O'Leary. She's our favorite children's mystery writer. Fiona invited us all to her huge mansion for the weekend. We were going to hear her read her new book, *The Cat's Meow*, out loud for the first time.

Ashley and I read mystery books all the time. Probably because we run the Olsen and Olsen Detective Agency from our attic. We *love* solving mysteries.

"Your great-grandmother's books are ter-rific, Patty," Ashley said. She leaned back against the velvety seat. "I especially like

Flapper—that fluffy white cat who's always in them."

Patty rolled her eyes. "Well, Flapper happens to be real," she said. "Great-grandmother never goes anywhere without that cat."

"I feel like I already know everything about Flapper," Ashley said. "In the books, she has a real satin bed. And a squeaky mouse toy that she always keeps next to her pillow."

"Yeah," I added. "And she has a real ruby and emerald collar. Not too shabby for a cat."

"Great-grandmother treats Flapper like a queen." Patty sniffed. She flipped her brown hair over her shoulder and frowned. "Whoever heard of a cat named Flapper, anyway? Cats don't have wings!"

Ashley shook her head. "The word 'flapper' comes from the 1920s," she explained. "It's what they used to call young women

who flapped their arms a lot when they danced."

"How do you know that?" Patty asked.

Ashley shrugged. "When I found out we were going to a real 1920s mansion, I did some research," she replied.

That didn't surprise me. Ashley and I look exactly alike, but we're different in one major way. Ashley likes to get all the facts before she makes a move. I move first, then get the facts!

"I wish Great-grandmother would spend more time with me," Patty said, staring out the window. "Like your great-grandmother does."

Our great-grandma Olive is the best. She spends tons of time with us. And she's also a fantastic detective! Ashley and I learned everything we know from her.

I sat back and smiled. The reading was just one of the fun things Fiona had planned. Since her book took place in the

1920s, there would be a Charleston contest one night. The Charleston was a dance everyone did back then. Fiona was going to give the winner a big silver trophy cup to take home.

"We're here!" Patty cried. "Great-grand-mother's mansion!"

The driver stopped the car in front of a huge white house. He held the door open as we all filed out.

"Wow!" I gasped as Ashley and I looked around. The house was surrounded by a beautiful red and white rose garden. And the hedges were trimmed to look like cats.

The driver carried our backpacks to the front door. Then he tipped his hat, got back into the car, and drove away.

Our exciting weekend was about to begin!

We walked up to the shiny, black front door. Patty reached out and rang the door-bell. After a few seconds a man wearing a

stiff-looking white suit opened the door.

"You all must be Miss Patricia and her friends," the man said, bowing slightly. "I am Madam O'Leary's butler, Martin."

I tried not to giggle. Martin's nose was so high in the air, he looked like he was sniffing something.

"I don't remember you," Patty said. "Are you new?"

"Indeed!" Martin said. "I am a recent graduate of the White Gloves Academy for the Butler Arts."

I looked at Martin's hands. He wasn't wearing white gloves. But he *was* wearing a flashy diamond pinky ring.

"Do come in," Martin said. He stepped back from the door. "Madam will greet you in the sitting room."

We laid our backpacks in the hall. Clue's paws made a clicking noise as we followed Martin across the sparkling black and white tile floor.

"Pretty fancy ring for a butler," Ashley whispered. She stared at Martin's pinky.

"You're telling me," I whispered back. "Mrs. O'Leary must pay him really well."

Martin opened a pair of double doors that led into the sitting room. We all stepped inside.

The bright sitting room had another pair of glass doors that opened out into a garden. The furniture was polished to a shine. And all the chairs were covered with flowered cloth that looked like silk.

"Madam will join you shortly," Martin said. "Would you care for some lemonade?"

"Yes, please," we all replied.

Martin picked up the lemonade pitcher and began to pour. But his hands shook a lot. More lemonade went onto the rug than into our glasses.

"Some butler," Patty grumbled. "He doesn't even know how to pour lemonade."

I took a sip from my glass and

scrunched up my face. He didn't know how to *make* lemonade either. It was so sour!

"Oh, look!" Ashley pointed across the room. "What a beautiful vase that is!"

I turned to see where Ashley was pointing. A tall white vase stood on the floor across the room. It had a colorful dragon painted on it.

"That's the biggest vase I've ever seen," I said.

"Tell me about it," Ashley replied. "It's as big as my desk at school!"

"That's my priceless Ming Dynasty vase," a voice said.

I turned and saw a woman standing at the double doors. She wore a pink suit and she was holding a fluffy white cat. The cat wore a ruby and emerald collar around her neck.

"Great-grandmother!" Patty cried happily. She ran toward her.

"Patricia, darling," Fiona O'Leary said,

smiling at Patty. But then her gaze shifted. Fiona looked straight at Clue.

"Oh no!" she shrieked. "A dog!"

The cat howled and jumped out of Fiona's arms. Then it dashed out of the sitting room.

"Flapper, come back to Mommy!" Fiona called. But it was too late. The cat was gone!

CATNAPPED!

Fiona turned and glared at Clue. "My precious has been scared away by that nasty *dog*!"

"I told them not to bring that dog, Great-grandmother," Patty said. "I told them!"

I shot Patty a surprised look. Some help *she* was.

"It's not Clue's fault, Mrs. O'Leary," Ashley said. "Flapper probably got scared when you raised your voice."

Fiona didn't answer for a moment. Then

she sighed. "Well, I suppose I was a bit surprised," she said. "After all, I never ever let my precious kitty near other animals."

"I'll see if I can find Miss Flapper for you, madam," Martin announced. He spun on his well-polished heel and marched out of the room.

Fiona turned to Ashley and me. "Well," she said, "it *is* very nice to meet the Trenchcoat Twins."

"We're pleased to meet you, too," Ashley said.

"And we can't wait to hear your new book," I added.

"Good!" Fiona said. "And you'll be happy to know that another young detective has already arrived. He's one of my *biggest* fans."

"Really?" I asked. It wasn't often that Ashley and I met other kid detectives.

At that moment, the double doors swung open. A boy with red hair and freckles

walked in. He was wearing a weird-looking pair of goggles with blinking lights.

He wobbled through the room and crashed into the dragon vase. It tipped over, about to fall.

Ashley ran over. She caught the vase just in time. "Phew!" she said. "That was close!"

The boy adjusted his goggles and grinned sheepishly. "Sorry," he said. "I was just testing my Daring Detective X-ray Scanning Device."

"Who are you, anyway?" Patty asked.

"Albert Von Shreck is my name," the boy said. "And state-of-the-art sleuthing is my game."

"Excuse me?" Ashley said.

"I belong to the Gumshoe Gadget-of-the-Month Club," Albert explained. "They send me all the things I need to crack a case."

"You mean like those goggles?" Patty asked.

"And these." Albert lifted his foot. "They

may *look* like average sneakers, but when I'm in a jam, they become walking walkie-talkies!"

Ashley and I looked at each other. Was this guy for real?

"I'm Ashley Olsen and this is my sister, Mary-Kate," Ashley said.

"Ah, the famous Trenchcoat Twins," Albert replied. "So what type of gadgets do *you* use?"

"Gadgets?" I asked. "Well, we use a tape recorder that our great-grandma gave us."

"And a pad and pencil," Ashley added.

"How prehistoric!" Albert scoffed.

Ashley and I exchanged glances again.

"I hate to disappoint you, Albert," Fiona said, "but there won't be much use for your gadgets this weekend."

Albert looked disappointed. "I wish there was a mystery to solve," he said.

MEOW!

I turned around. A blond woman dressed

in a black dress and a white apron stood in the doorway. She was holding Flapper in her arms.

"Miss Flapper was in the pantry, madam," the woman said.

"Thank you for finding her," Fiona said. Then she ran over and took her cat. "There's my puffy, fluffy angel!" she cried.

Finally, Fiona looked up again. "This is my maid, Shirley," she told us. "Her most important job is taking care of Flapper."

Shirley nodded. "I'll get Miss Flapper's lunch ready now," she said. "But before I do, I was hoping to talk to you about my vacation."

"Vacation?" Fiona repeated. "You can't possibly take a vacation. I need you here to take care of my baby."

"B-but—" Shirley stammered.

"Now, don't forget," Fiona interrupted. "When you make Flapper her lunch, make sure to use only the freshest chicken we have in the refrigerator."

Shirley seemed to force a smile. "Yes, madam," she said. She took Flapper and hurried out of the room.

Clue wagged her tail and followed them. Luckily Fiona didn't seem to notice. I don't think she wanted Clue anywhere near Flapper.

"The reading will take place in an hour," Fiona announced. "Patricia, why don't you show our detectives around?"

"Count me out," Albert said. He pointed to his feet. "My walkie-talkie sneakers are picking up signals."

"Of a mystery?" I asked.

Albert shook his head. "I think it's the Dodgers game," he said.

As we were leaving the room, Fiona called, "There are intercoms in every room. Feel free to call if you need anything."

Patty led us both down a long, carpeted hallway. She quickly walked past the large

paintings of Flapper that lined the walls.

"This house was built in the early 1900s," Patty said. "It belonged to a jewel thief called Shifty-Eyes Malone."

A 1920s song had started playing somewhere nearby. "Where's that music coming from?" I asked.

"Probably the ballroom," Patty answered. We walked down the hallway to the ballroom and peeked inside. The room was huge, with the tallest windows I'd ever seen. A sparkly crystal chandelier hung from the center of the ceiling.

Then we saw Martin. He was shaking his way around the polished dance floor, dancing the Charleston.

"A dancing butler!" I giggled.

Martin flapped his hands so fast that his diamond ring slid off his pinky. It flew across the room. He didn't seem to see us as he ran to pick it up.

"That ring must be pretty loose," Ashley

said. "If I had a ring like that, I'd make *sure* it stayed on tight."

"Well, he'd better get back to work," Patty huffed.

She led us to our room. It was just as fancy as the rest of the house. It had two poster beds, a white dresser, and frilly curtains covering the windows. An intercom with black and green buttons hung next to the door.

"Cool," Ashley said.

"I'm going back down to see Great-grandmother," Patty said. "See you later."

"See you," I replied. But I was looking at a painting hanging over the dresser. It showed a man wearing a white fedora hat and a pinstripe suit. His deep-set eyes seemed to shift back and forth.

"That *has* to be Shifty-Eyes Malone," I said.

"Check out that stickpin he's wearing," Ashley added nodding toward the portrait.

I walked over to get a closer look. There were three big diamonds on the tip of the pin, and a bunch of smaller diamonds.

"The jewels form the shape of an 'M,'" I said. "Probably for Malone."

Ashley tilted her head as she studied the painting. "There's something familiar about Shifty," she said slowly. "It's like I've seen him somewhere before."

"Impossible." I pointed to a tiny gold plate on the frame. "It says that Shifty died in 1978. That's before we were born."

Ashley shrugged. "It was just a weird feeling, I guess," she said. Then she ran across the room.

"Ohmigosh, look at this!" she cried. She pointed to a tall wooden box by the window. "It's a Victrola."

"A what-ola?" I asked.

Ashley lifted the lid. "It's what they used to call record players in the 1920s," she explained. "Way before CD players."

I grinned. Ashley's research was really paying off. I was learning a lot!

"Come on, Mary-Kate." Ashley placed a record on the turntable and cranked up the Victrola. "Let's practice for the Charleston contest."

"Yes, sir, that's my baby!" a scratchy voice sang as the record spun. "No, sir! Don't mean maybe!"

Ashley and I danced around the room, pretending to be flappers. We were interrupted by a loud beep.

"Yes?" I asked, pressing the intercom button.

"Madam requests your presence in the library," Martin's voice said.

"The reading!" Ashley and I said at the same time. We were so excited, we ran all the way to the library.

Fiona was standing at the front of the room. "Where are Patricia and Albert?" she asked. She looked over her reading glasses.

"And where is my kitty angel? I never read without Flapper at my side."

The doors burst open. Ashley and I spun around. Albert and Patty had arrived. Albert was carrying a briefcase with the words "Gumshoe Gadgets" written on the front.

"I charged up my Incredible Crime-Stopping Chronometer," he said, holding up his wrist.

"Looks like a plain old watch to me," I whispered to Ashley.

"Sorry I'm late, Great-grandmother," Patty said. She took a seat. "I was up in my room unpacking."

The library doors swung open again. This time it was Shirley. She looked very scared.

"Shirley?" Fiona asked. "Is something wrong?"

"Yes, madam!" Shirley cried. "It's Miss Flapper. She's...she's...missing!"

DOGGONE GUILTY

Missing? I stared at Ashley. That's a serious word to detectives like us!

"I was giving Miss Flapper her strawberry bubble bath," Shirley explained. "And Martin called me on the intercom from the kitchen. He asked me to bring him some fresh towels from the laundry room."

"So you left Flapper alone?" Fiona sounded shocked.

"N-n-not exactly," Shirley stammered. "That basset hound was in the room, too."

I shot another glance at Ashley. Shirley was talking about Clue!

"I was gone only about fifteen minutes," Shirley continued. She looked close to tears. "I even made sure the door to Miss Flapper's room was closed. But when I came back—she was gone."

"Awesome!" Patty blurted out. Then she clapped a hand over her mouth. "I mean...how awful."

"I'm so sorry, ma'am," Shirley said. "I've looked everywhere." She wiped away a tear and ran out of the room.

Fiona grabbed onto a chair. "My baby...gone? It just can't be."

"A missing cat!" Albert cried. "This sounds like a job for Albert Von Shreck."

"Cool your jets, Albert," Ashley said. "Flapper is probably hiding somewhere in her room."

"Come on," I said. "Let's go there and find out right now."

Everyone dashed out of the library and up the stairs. As I ran by a half-closed door, I heard a woman's voice chatting to someone. Ashley must have heard it, too. We both stopped.

We peeked inside the room. Shirley was talking on the phone.

"Can you believe it, Felicia?" Shirley was saying. "Flapper is gone. I am so excited!"

Excited? My mouth dropped open.

"That's right, Felicia," Shirley went on. "I'm finally free. Vacation, here I come."

I glanced at Ashley. Shirley wasn't crying anymore. In fact, she looked totally happy!

"Too weird," Ashley whispered, as we quickly joined the others. They were already in Flapper's room.

"This room is just like the one in Fiona's books," I told Ashley in a low voice. There was a blue satin kitty bed, a white furry scratching post, and a miniature bathtub surrounded by bottles of bubble bath.

And Clue was sitting in the middle of the room.

"What is that dog still doing in here?" Fiona asked. "She probably chased my precious out the open window."

"Her name is Clue," Ashley said. "And she does not chase cats."

"We haven't even looked for Flapper yet," I added. "I'm sure she'll turn up somewhere."

"Don't bother looking," Albert said. He was holding a long metal rod with a blinking light at the end.

"What is that?" I asked.

"It's my Sonar Suspect Scepter!" Albert declared. "It beeps when I wave it over a suspect." He waved the crazy-looking gizmo over Clue.

"Hello? It's not beeping," Ashley pointed out.

"That's...um...because it only beeps over the innocent," Albert said. He pointed a finger at Clue. "Guilty as charged!"

"How could you do it?" Fiona scolded. She shook her finger at Clue.

"Yeah!" Patty added, moving closer to Fiona.

Clue whined and lay down on the rug. She covered her droopy face with her paws.

"Let's not blame Clue," Ashley said. "Let's hunt for Flapper instead."

"Ashley's right," I said. "Let's spread out and search the grounds and the house. We can meet back in Flapper's room in an hour."

"You mean fifty-nine minutes and forty-five seconds," Albert said. "That's according to my Crime-Stopping—"

"Chronometer." I sighed. "We know, we know."

Everyone else split up to look for Flapper, but Ashley and I stuck together.

We searched the house from top to bottom. We looked around the grounds and even the tennis courts. There was no sign of Flapper anywhere.

"I hate to admit it, Ashley," I said, "but it looks like somebody *did* get rid of Flapper."

"If that's the case," Ashley said, "then the Trenchcoat Twins have a case to solve."

"No luck," I announced when we gathered again in Flapper's room.

I could tell the others hadn't found Flapper, either. They looked sad and serious. Except Albert. He looked psyched.

"I knew it!" he declared. "Clue chased Flapper out the window and she ran away."

"What am I going to do?" Fiona wailed.

"Poor Great-grandmother," Patty cooed. "What you need is a nice cup of warm milk. And cookies. Then we can play Go Fish, to take your mind off things." She gently led Fiona out of the room.

"Looks like you two had better start packing," Albert told Ashley and me. "And don't forget your trenchcoats."

"We're not going anywhere," I said. "Ashley and I are going to find Flapper and prove that Clue is innocent."

Albert shrugged. He followed us as we walked over to the window. I leaned over and checked out the windowsill.

"Hmmm," I said. "The dust here hasn't been touched."

Ashley nodded. "If Flapper jumped out the window, she would have left wet paw prints from her bath."

I heard Albert clear his throat. I turned around. He was wearing a pair of glasses with spinning spirals.

"What are those?" I demanded.

"They're my Secret Spy's Eyes," Albert replied. "With them, I can see what the average eye misses."

Albert walked around the room. He kept

bumping into furniture. He finally decided to take the glasses off when he fell into the kitty bed.

"Aha," he said. He picked a piece of pink yarn off the blue satin. "A clue!"

Ashley and I looked at each other. Albert actually *had* found a clue.

"Maybe Shirley knows where that came from," Ashley said.

"Let's go find her," Albert said. We all dashed into the hallway. Shirley was coming toward us. She was holding some kind of brochure in front of her face. More brochures were stuffed under her arm.

"Shirley!" I called.

"Huh?" Shirley gasped. Startled, she dropped the papers all over the floor.

I reached down to help her pick them up. They were lots of travel brochures—India, China, Argentina. If Shirley was planning to leave town, she was going to do it in a big way.

"What do you want?" Shirley asked nervously, as I handed her the brochures.

"Does this look familiar?" Albert asked. He dangled the pink string in front of Shirley's face.

"That looks like yarn from the booties Miss Flapper wears after her bath," Shirley answered. "Excuse me, but I'm in a hurry." She hugged the papers to her chest and ran down the hall.

"No wonder there were no wet paw prints on the windowsill," Albert said smugly. "Flapper was wearing booties."

"Even if she was wearing booties she would have left some kind of marks on the windowsill," I told Albert.

He ignored me. "Maybe Clue was jealous of Flapper's nice things," he went on. "And it drove her to crime!"

"Oh, please." I laughed. "Clue doesn't care about bubble baths and satin beds."

The three of us returned to Flapper's

room to look for more clues. But when we opened the door, Ashley and I both froze.

There, stretched out on Flapper's satin bed, was Clue. Her ears flopped over the bed as she gave a lazy yawn.

Albert folded his arms. "See, I was right. I've solved the case!"

4

A NOISY CLUE

"**T**his doesn't mean a thing," I insisted.

"In your dreams," Albert replied. He smiled smugly and left Flapper's room.

"Um, since when does Clue like satin beds?" Ashley asked me in a low voice.

"Who wouldn't?" I replied. "But that doesn't mean she chased Flapper out the window."

"Well, we'd better clear Clue's name—fast," Ashley said. "Because right now we're the only ones who think she's innocent."

We left Clue snoozing on the bed. It was time to get back to our room and get to work.

"Okay," Ashley said. She sat down next to me on my bed. "What do we know so far?"

"We know that Shirley said the door to Flapper's room was closed when she disappeared," I said. "So the cat couldn't have left through the door."

"Not on her own," Ashley added. "But maybe she was taken out of the room by someone."

"Who would have taken Flapper?" I wondered out loud.

Ashley took her detective notebook out of her backpack. She opened it to a clean page and wrote the word "Suspects."

"Patty doesn't like Flapper," I said, "because her great-grandma spends too much time with her."

"And Patty was late for the reading,"

Ashley pointed out. "That's about when Flapper disappeared."

"Maybe Patty got rid of Flapper so she could get her great-grandma's attention," I said. "I think she's a pretty good suspect."

Ashley wrote Patty's name in her notebook. Then she tapped her chin with the pencil. "What about Albert?" she asked. "He really wanted to work on a mystery so he could show off his silly gadgets. And he was late for the reading, too."

I watched as Ashley wrote Albert's name under Patty's.

"Both of them said they were in their rooms," I said. "So it might be hard to check their stories."

"What about Shirley?" I asked. "She sure seemed happy after Flapper disappeared."

Ashley nodded. "And now she's free to take that vacation."

"Shirley could have gotten rid of Flapper during bath time," I suggested. "And then

used Martin's call as an excuse."

I pulled my tape recorder from my backpack. "Let's go back to Flapper's room," I said. "We need more evidence."

But when we got to Flapper's room, we weren't alone. Albert was dusting a bright pink powder all over Flapper's bed.

"What are you doing?" I asked. "And where is Clue?"

"Your dog wasn't here when I came in," Albert said. He stood up holding the cardboard box of powder. "I wanted to dust for prints with my supersensitive Daring Detective Dust."

Albert held the box in front of my face. My nose began to twitch. Then I let out a big sneeze.

"Ah-choooo!"

Albert yelped as pink powder flew everywhere.

"Look what you did." Albert coughed under the cloud of pink dust. "Now we'll never know if the dust works."

"Trust me, it *wouldn't*," I muttered.

While Albert tried to scoop up the pink powder, Ashley and I searched the room. The rug was shaggy, so it was hard to look for footprints.

Ashley stopped by the satin bed.

"What's the matter?" I asked.

"Something isn't right," Ashley said. Then her eyes lit up. "I know! The squeaky mouse toy that Flapper keeps in the corner of her bed isn't there."

"How do you know she had a mouse toy?" Albert asked.

"From Fiona's books," Ashley said. She planted her hands on her hips. "I thought you were her biggest fan."

"Maybe Flapper ran away on her own," I suggested. "And took her toy with her."

"Or maybe Clue took it," Albert said, "because she wanted Flapper's cool toys."

"Clue doesn't play with squeaky toys," I

insisted. "She's strictly a stuffed-thing dog."

I pressed the record button on my tape recorder. Then I said, "Clue number one: Squeaky mouse toy is missing from its usual spot."

I was about to say more when Albert grabbed the tape recorder. "Let me see that," he said.

He played back the message I had just recorded.

"Clue number one: Squeaky mouse toy is missing—"

"Why is the tape squeaking?" Ashley asked.

"The squeaking isn't coming from the tape," I said. I clicked off the tape recorder.

We all listened closely.

SQUEAK...SQUEAK...SQUEAK.

"It's coming from the hall," Ashley said.

"Wait!" Albert said. He pulled something out of his briefcase. It was a pair of earphones that looked like long fox ears. "I need my Super-Sleuth Sound-Sensitive Ears."

Ashley and I rolled our eyes.

SQUEAK...SQUEAK.

The noise got louder as we walked down the hall. We followed the sound into one of the bedrooms.

The door was halfway open.

"Flapper?" I called. "Are you in there?"

CAUGHT IN THE ACT

I opened the door, but I didn't see Flapper. Instead I saw Clue sitting in the middle of the room.

"What are you doing in here?" I asked.

Clue shifted.

SQUEAK.

"Oh, no," Ashley said. "The squeaking noise is coming from under Clue!"

We struggled to pick up our dog. It wasn't easy. She didn't seem to want to move. Finally we saw why Clue wanted to stay put.

"Look!" Albert exclaimed. He pointed to the mouse squeak toy on the rug. "Clue was hiding Flapper's toy. I knew she took it."

"Our dog is a detective," Ashley declared. "She doesn't commit crimes. She *solves* them."

"A dog detective?" Albert laughed. "I'll believe it when I see it."

"Okay then," Ashley said. She picked Clue up. "Come with me."

Ashley called Shirley, Patty, and Fiona into the library. I had no idea what my sister had up her sleeve.

"What is the meaning of this, girls?" Fiona asked.

"Yeah," Patty said. "We were busy looking at the family album."

Ashley folded her arms. "My sister and I want to announce that we will not be solving this case alone."

"Yes!" Albert cheered. "You finally admit that you can't get the job done without

the help of Albert Von Shreck!"

"No," Ashley said. "We're going to solve this crime with our silent partner. Our dog Clue."

I grinned. Ashley was going to clear Clue's name by having her help solve the case!

"You can't use Clue!" Patty exclaimed. "She's a suspect."

"She's a detective and we'll prove it," Ashley said. "But first we'll need something special that belongs to Flapper."

"Here," Shirley said. She handed Ashley a folded piece of cloth. "I was just about to wash Miss Flapper's kitty bib."

"Thanks," Ashley said. "Now all I have to do is give this to Clue to sniff. Then she'll lead us to Flapper."

She pressed the bib against Clue's nose. "Here, girl," she said. "Take us to Flapper."

Clue didn't move.

"This is a waste of time." Fiona sighed.

Then Clue gave a short bark. She dashed out of the room.

"Go, Clue!" Ashley and I cheered as we all ran after her.

"She's heading toward the kitchen," Fiona said. "Maybe Flapper is in there."

But when we reached the kitchen, we froze. Clue hadn't led us to Flapper. She had led us to Flapper's kitty dish! And now she was gobbling up freshly cooked chicken.

"Your case isn't looking so good, *detectives*," Albert said. "What are you going to do now?"

6

CLUE SMELLS GUILTY

Ashley defended our dog. "Clue was just following the scent of the chicken on the kitty bib," she said.

Fiona looked at us sharply. "All evidence does seem to point to Clue," she said.

"Please, Mrs. O'Leary," Ashley said. "Let us prove Clue didn't do it. We know we can find Flapper if we just have a little more time."

"No," Fiona said. "I'm too upset now. I want everyone to go home."

"But we just got here!" Patty said.

"And we still really want to enter the Charleston contest," I added quickly. "We've both been practicing really hard."

"Okay. You can all stay, but I'm afraid there will be no contest if Flapper isn't found," Fiona said sadly.

Martin suddenly appeared in the doorway. "Lunch will be served in the main dining room," he announced.

Ashley and I took Clue to our bedroom. We put her on the rug and shut the door. Then we walked back downstairs to the dining room.

Fiona was seated at the head of the table. "Martin, would you please toss the salad?" she asked the butler.

Martin looked confused. "Are you sure you want me to do that?" he replied.

"Of course I am," Fiona responded. "Go ahead."

"Okay." Martin shrugged. Then he reached into the big salad bowl and began

throwing lettuce across the table.

"What are you doing?" Fiona shrieked. A piece of cucumber flew past her head.

"But, madam, you said to toss the salad," Martin said.

I leaned over to Ashley. "This guy is definitely *not* butler material," I whispered.

Luckily, lunch went pretty smoothly after that. We ate tiny sandwiches with the crusts cut off. For dessert Shirley served fresh fruit.

After lunch Fiona and Patty went outside to play croquet. Albert hurried upstairs to play with his gadgets. Ashley and I got back to work.

We decided to search the house again. Charleston music floated out from the ballroom as we walked past. Martin was inside, kicking his legs and waving his arms.

"Look," I whispered. "Martin is doing the Charleston again. He must be entering the dance contest."

We watched as Martin's ring flew off his finger for the second time.

I shook my head. "Martin might win the contest," I said. "But if he isn't more careful, he's going to lose that ring."

We headed upstairs to check all the bedrooms. Shirley's voice was coming from inside Flapper's room. Ashley and I peeked inside.

"I can't believe it," Ashley gasped in a low voice.

Clue was sitting in Flapper's white bathtub. She was surrounded by a cloud of bubbles, and she was even wearing a pink frilly shower cap. Shirley was giving our dog a bubble bath!

"Good doggy," Shirley was saying. "Now you'll smell just like that hairball of a cat."

Ashley and I ducked away from the door and looked at each other.

"If Shirley *did* get rid of Flapper," I said, "then maybe she's trying to make Clue

seem guilty. I bet that's what happened."

"We have no proof of that," Ashley said. "Besides, we still have two other suspects to deal with: Albert and Patty."

"Albert ran right upstairs after lunch," I said. "I wonder what he's doing."

"Let's check it out," Ashley suggested. "Which room is his?"

We had no trouble figuring out the answer to that one. Albert's room had a sign on the door that read GUMSHOE GENIUS AT WORK!

Ashley knocked on the door.

No answer.

"Hello?" I called, pushing open the door. Albert's room was fancy like ours. It had a thick carpet, a poster bed, and polished furniture. The only difference was this room had a big flowering plant by the window.

"Wow, look at all these gadgets," Ashley said. She pointed to a pile of goggles, telescopes, and mini-radios on Albert's bed.

I saw the goofy fox ears Albert had been wearing earlier and put them on.

"Testing! Testing one, two, three!" I giggled, wiggling the fake ears.

But Ashley wasn't laughing. Her face was pale as she pointed over my shoulder.

"What is it?" I asked, pulling off the ears.

"M-M-Mary-Kate!" Ashley stammered. "Look!"

I turned around. Then I froze.

The plant by the window was walking toward us!

THE CAT'S OUT
OF THE BAG

"**A**uugghh!" Ashley and I screamed. We started to run away.

"Thought you could spy on me, huh?" a voice called.

I turned back. I recognized that pesky voice.

"Albert?" Ashley said, leaning forward. Sure enough, there was his face, peeking out from between the flowers and leaves.

"Guess you were fooled by my undercover shrub disguise," Albert declared.

I folded my arms over my chest. "Why'd you have to scare us like that?" I asked.

"I was going to use this disguise to stake out the mansion," Albert explained. "But when I heard you two sneaking into my room, I figured I'd give it a test run."

"Very funny," Ashley said. "See you later, Albert."

On the way back downstairs, I heard another strange noise. It was coming from the sitting room.

"Ashley!" I whispered. "Do you hear that?"

"Hear what?" Ashley asked. She was looking at Fiona's Ming Dynasty vase across the room.

"I could have sworn that dragon head was facing out the last time we saw it," she said.

I knew what Ashley meant. This time the dragon's *tail* was on the front of the vase. "Someone must have moved it," I said.

We walked over to the vase. That's when I heard the strange noise again.

It came from inside the Ming Dynasty vase. And this time Ashley heard it, too.

MEOW.

We both peered into the tall vase. There was Flapper, curled up on the bottom. She was looking up at us with big wide eyes.

"Flapper!" Ashley and I shouted at the same time.

I leaned down to lift her out, but I couldn't reach her. The vase was too deep. "There's no way Flapper could have climbed in there," I said.

"Did someone say Flapper?" Fiona cried, running into the room. Patty was right behind her.

"We sure did," I said. "Flapper is inside this vase. Someone must have put her there."

Fiona and Patty looked inside the vase. Tears of joy filled Fiona's eyes. But Patty did *not* look happy at all.

"I'm going to tell everyone else," Fiona said. "They'll all be so thrilled!" She swept out of the room.

"How should we get Flapper out?" Ashley asked.

"Put the vase on the carpet and tip it," Patty said. "It's a lot easier to reach her that way."

I raised my eyebrows. "You seem pretty sure of that, Patty," I said.

Patty didn't respond.

The three of us carefully placed the vase on the floor. Ashley and I tipped the vase. Then Patty reached in to grab Flapper. As her sleeves moved up, I noticed long red marks on both of her arms.

"How did you get those scratches, Patty?" I asked.

Patty's eyes got wide. She quickly pulled down her sleeves. "Scratches?" she asked. "I don't see any scratches."

"Hmmm," Ashley said. "They sort of look like they were made by…a cat."

"Patty," I asked, "why did you put Flapper in the vase?"

"I didn't," Patty snapped.

Ashley and I just stood there, looking at her.

"Okay!" she confessed. "I did it. And I'd do it again. For once Great-grandmother is paying attention to *me*."

I glanced at Ashley. The cat was still in the vase, but it was definitely out of the bag.

"Hey, I slipped the hairball some food from time to time," Patty went on. "I was going to take her out before I went home."

"Patty, you worried your great-grandma sick," Ashley scolded.

"And," I added, "you let Clue take the blame!"

"You won't tell Great-grandmother, will you?" Patty pleaded.

"We won't tell." Ashley sighed. "But don't

do anything like this again."

"I won't," Patty promised.

Ashley and I watched as Patty pulled Flapper out of the vase. Then she handed the cat to me.

"Hi, Flapper." I scratched Flapper gently around her neck. That's when I noticed that something wasn't right.

"Flapper isn't wearing her jeweled collar," I said.

"Patty," Ashley asked slowly, "did you take the collar?"

"No!" Patty insisted. "Flapper wasn't even wearing her collar when I stuffed her inside the vase."

"Looks like we have another mystery on our hands," I said. "Figuring out who stole Flapper's fancy collar."

"Missing jewels are serious," Ashley said. "We'd better tell Fiona."

"No!" Patty begged. "She'll call the police. And they'll figure out that I'm the

one who put Flapper in the vase."

"Well, what do you want us to do?" I asked Patty.

"Maybe you can find the collar before Great-grandmother realizes it's gone," Patty said. "Can't you just try?"

"Fine," Ashley told Patty. "But if we don't find the collar by tomorrow morning we'll *have* to tell Fiona."

"Okay," Patty said. "I guess that's fair."

Ashley and I looked at each other. We had cracked the case and found Flapper. But could we solve case number two by tomorrow morning?

8

ANOTHER MYSTERY!

Ashley and I went upstairs to our room. We had to answer the big question. Who would want to steal Flapper's collar?

I pointed to the portrait of Shifty-Eyes Malone. "He'd probably know," I said. "He was a jewel thief."

Ashley sighed and crossed Patty's name from our suspect list. "Only two suspects left," she said.

"Albert is still a suspect," I said. "He could have taken the necklace to create a

mystery here that he could solve."

"And let's not forget Shirley," Ashley added. "Remember those travel brochures? Maybe she stole the collar so that she could pay for all those vacations."

We were interrupted by a knock on the door. It was Albert.

"I heard you found Flapper," he said. "Sorry I kept saying it was your dog."

"No problem," I said, shrugging. "But there's still a mystery to solve. Flapper's collar is missing. Do you want to help us find it?"

"Sure!" Albert said.

Ashley grabbed my arm and pulled me to the other side of the room. "What are you thinking?" she whispered. "Albert is still a suspect."

"Exactly," I whispered. "And this way we can keep him close by us at all times."

Ashley thought about that. "It just might work," she said.

We went back over to Albert. "Let's get to work," I said. "We'll start by investigating Shirley."

The three of us found Fiona's maid in Flapper's room. She was brushing the cat with a silver brush and muttering under her breath.

"Let's question her right now," Ashley whispered.

"No need to," Albert said. "When Flapper disappeared, I secretly put a tube of Truth-paste in everyone's bathroom. If Shirley is guilty, her teeth will be bright blue."

"That's the dumbest thing I've ever heard." Ashley laughed.

Shirley turned around. "What do you kids want out there?" she asked.

I couldn't stop staring at her mouth as she talked. It was totally blue!

"I told you!" Albert cried. "The truth is in the tooth. Guilty as charged."

"What are you talking about?" Shirley

asked. She crossed her arms.

"Your teeth are all blue, thanks to my trusty Truth-paste," Albert declared.

"My teeth are blue because I had blueberry pie with my tea," Shirley said. "What do you mean, 'guilty as charged'?"

I gave Ashley a nod. She took a deep breath.

"Shirley?" she asked. "Did you steal something that you want to tell us about?"

Shirley's mouth dropped open. She twisted her apron between her hands.

"Yes, I did," she admitted slowly. "And I'd steal it again!"

9

THE EYES HAVE IT

"**S**o it was *you* who stole the kitty collar!" Albert said excitedly. "I knew it the whole time."

"What kitty collar?" Shirley asked. "I stole Flapper's squeaky mouse toy."

The room was silent.

"The…squeaky toy?" I repeated.

"I stole it for Clue," Shirley said. "As a reward."

"Why should Clue get a reward?" I asked, confused.

"Because," Shirley said, "I wanted to give her something nice for chasing Flapper out of the house."

Flapper hissed.

"I also put Clue on Flapper's bed to relax," Shirley went on. "And I gave her one of Flapper's strawberry bubble baths."

It suddenly hit me like a ton of kitty litter. No wonder Clue seemed so guilty. Without knowing it, Shirley had framed our dog! "Framed" is a detective word. It means making someone look guilty.

"Shirley," Ashley asked. "Where were you when Flapper disappeared?"

"Down in the kitchen," Shirley said. "I brought Martin those towels he needed from the laundry room."

"Was Martin in the kitchen, too?" Ashley asked.

"Yes," Shirley said.

"Thanks for the information," I told her. "We have to go now."

The three of us walked back into the hall. Ashley and I walked slowly, thinking hard. But Albert began to run.

"Where are you going?" Ashley called.

"To get one of my gadgets," Albert called back.

"Wait!" I shouted as we chased Albert down the hall. "We don't need your—"

SLAM!

Ashley and I rounded a corner and crashed right into Martin. The silver platter of party favors he was holding clattered to the floor.

"Sorry," I said. "We'll help you pick them up."

"That won't be necessary," Martin said. Then his eyes shifted slowly from Ashley to me.

Wait a minute, I thought. *Shifty!*

"Um, whatever you say," I told Martin quickly. Then I grabbed Ashley's arm and dragged her to our room.

"Guess what!" I cried after I shut the door. "I know why Shifty-Eyes Malone looked so familiar. Martin has the exact same shifty look as the guy in the portrait."

"I noticed that, too," Ashley said. "Do you think there's some connection between Martin and Shifty-Eyes Malone?"

"I don't know." I gulped. I looked up at the portrait. "But Shifty's eyes look even shiftier now."

A knock on the door made us jump.

"It's me," Albert called. "Open up."

Ashley opened the door. Albert jumped into our room holding a long metal rod. "Ta-da," he announced. "It's my Tried and True Metal Detector."

"A metal detector?" I repeated. "I've seen people use those things on the beach. It helps them find coins and lost jewelry."

"Exactly!" Albert cried. "And the band on the kitty collar was made out of gold. That's a metal, right?"

I nodded. I couldn't believe it. For once Albert had a useful gadget!

"That's not from your Gumshoe Gadget-of-the-Month Club is it?" Ashley asked.

"Nope," Albert said. "It was a present from my grandma Ida. So I could find the gold tooth she lost."

"Let's go for it," I cheered.

Albert shoved the metal detector into my hands. "*You* go for it," he said. "I'm going to find some of that blueberry pie."

Ashley and I stared at Albert as he ran down the hall.

"What are we going to do now?" I asked.

"What else?" Ashley grinned. "Search for gold."

Holding the metal detector in front of me, I walked through the house. Ashley was right behind me.

BEEP! BEEP! BEEP!

I clutched the rod and gasped. It was beeping next to a tall wooden chest in the

dining room. Was this the place?

Ashley opened the chest. There on the shelf was a silver tea service. "Silver is a metal, too." She sighed.

Next, we entered the ballroom. The metal detector beeped as I walked toward a wood table. The silver trophy cup for the dance contest stood on top.

Ashley picked up the cup and cradled it in her arms. "I really hope I win this," she said.

I giggled as my sister strutted around the ballroom pretending to thank imaginary judges.

Ashley stopped mid–thank you as she stared into the silver trophy cup. "Mary-Kate," she cried. "You'll never believe what's in here!"

FINDING THE PRIZE

I hurried over to peek inside. "Wow!" I gasped. Flapper's fancy cat collar was at the bottom of the cup. "Not only did we find silver—we found gold, too!"

"Why would the thief put the collar inside the trophy cup?" Ashley asked.

"Maybe the thief was planning to win the dance contest tonight," I said. "Then he or she could take the cup and the collar home and—"

"No one would ever know," Ashley fin-

ished for me. She stepped forward to put the trophy back on the table and almost tripped.

"Are you okay?" I asked.

"I just stepped on something," Ashley replied, looking at the floor.

I looked down, too. My sister had stepped on a ring—a diamond pinky ring!

Ashley picked it up. "This is Martin's," she said. "He must have dropped it again while he was dancing."

I gave a low whistle as I gazed at the diamonds on the ring. They formed the letter *M*.

"Ashley, check it out," I said. "The diamonds on the ring look exactly like the ones Shifty-Eyes Malone was wearing in his portrait."

"You mean the ones on the stickpin?" Ashley asked.

"Yes!" I exclaimed. "Do you think they could be...the same diamonds?"

"I don't know," Ashley said, frowning. "The name Martin starts with an *M*, too. Besides, why would Martin want to steal the—"

I held up a hand. "Shhh!" I whispered. "Listen!"

"When the red, red robin comes bob-bob-bobbin' along!" a voice was singing. "There'll be no more sobbin—"

"I'll bet that's Martin now," I said. I picked up the collar and stuffed it into my jeans pocket. Ashley slipped the pinky ring into her shirt pocket.

Then we left the ballroom and followed the sound of music. It led us straight to the library.

I opened the double doors. Sure enough, there was Martin. He was dancing the Charleston next to a big boom box.

"He really wants to win that trophy," I whispered. "Maybe he *did* steal the collar."

"Wait," Ashley said. "Martin was in the

kitchen when the crime occurred. He called Shirley on the intercom. He couldn't have stolen the collar."

"Unless," I said slowly, "Martin *didn't* call Shirley from the kitchen."

Ashley's eyes lit up. "You're right! Fiona told us that all the rooms in the house have intercoms."

"Shirley gives Flapper a bath at the same time each day," I added. "She probably takes the cat's collar off, too. Maybe Martin called her from another room close to Flapper's. Then when Shirley left Flapper alone to go to the kitchen, Martin slipped into the room and grabbed the cat's collar!"

"That could be why Martin told Shirley to go to the laundry room first," Ashley said. "So he'd have plenty of time to steal the collar and then run down to the kitchen."

"It also gave Patty enough time to slip

into the room right after Martin and snatch Flapper," I said.

Ashley didn't answer. She was too busy thinking. "I have a plan," she said. "And it will tell us for sure if Martin is the thief!"

11

THE SET UP

"Did they really dress like this in the 1920s?" I asked Ashley that night. We were getting into our flapper outfits.

Ashley nodded. She was wearing a red fringed dress and a pearl choker. Her red hat fitted snugly over her hair.

My costume was awesome, too. I was wearing a purple dress and a jeweled head-band with feathers.

Even Clue was all dressed up, in a little purple hat and beads.

"These costumes Fiona loaned us are perfect," Ashley declared. "We look like real flappers now."

When we went downstairs, we saw that the other guests had already arrived. They were mostly grown-ups dressed in 1920s costumes.

"Welcome!" Fiona told everyone in the ballroom. She was wearing a beaded dress and a headpiece with a huge feather. She held a swingy beaded purse in one hand, and Flapper in the other.

Patty and Albert were snacking on cookies in the shape of feathers and fruit punch. Patty was dressed in a light blue dress and hat. Albert was wearing baggy pants, a sweater, and—of course—his walkie-talkie sneakers.

"This party is way cool," I told Ashley.

Just then I spotted Martin carrying a platter of cupcakes with vanilla and chocolate frosting. He was wearing a white hat

and a dark, sharp-looking pinstripe suit.

"Wow," Ashley said. "In that outfit, Martin looks just like Shifty-Eyes Malone."

"Attention, everyone!" Fiona announced. She stood in front of a window with the trophy cup in her hands. "It's time for the big dance contest to begin."

Shirley cranked up the old Victrola. A scratchy voice began to sing: "Charleston! Charleston!"

Everyone moved to the middle of the dance floor. Arms flapped, knees waved, and heels kicked.

"If I flapped any more, I'd fly!" I shouted to Ashley.

We all had a great time. But Martin was trying really hard. He was flying around the dance floor. He even did a split!

When the music ended, Ashley and I fell into each other's arms, laughing. "That was so much fun!" I said breathlessly.

"You were all fabulous," Fiona told us.

"As they would say in the 1920s—the cat's pajamas. But there can only be one winner. And the winner is—"

I sneaked a quick glance at Martin. He had a smug look on his face.

"—Ashley Burke!" Fiona announced.

"What?" Martin exploded. "That kid had nothing on me. *I* should be the winner of this contest!"

"I won! I won!" Ashley cheered. She took the silver trophy from Fiona. "I can't believe it."

I watched as Ashley began to stagger under the weight of the heavy cup. "Whoops!" she cried, as she tipped it out the window.

"Oh, no!" Martin cried. He headed for the double glass doors. "Excuse me, but the…um…mini hot dogs are ready."

"Come on, everyone," I called as Martin dashed out the doors. "Follow that butler!"

Ashley and I ran outside, with everyone

else behind us. We found Martin right where we expected him to be. He was on his hands and knees in the garden, under the open ballroom window.

"Hey, Martin," I called. "Can we help you find something?"

12

A PURR-FECT ENDING

Martin whipped around and stared at all of us. "Umm…no thanks. I was just—"

"Looking for *this*?" I said. I held up Flapper's jeweled collar.

"Hey, where did you—" Martin began.

"Or maybe you were looking for *this*," Ashley said. She held out the fancy pinky ring. "Tell us, how do you happen to have the same diamonds that Shifty-Eyes Malone wore on his stickpin?"

Everyone gasped in surprise.

Martin just stood there for a second with his mouth hanging open. Then he turned and began to run.

"He's getting away!" Fiona cried.

"That's what *you* think," Albert said. He whipped something out of his pocket that looked like a yo-yo. Then he aimed it at Martin. The string zipped out of the yo-yo and circled Martin like a cowboy's lasso.

"It's a good thing I happened to be carrying my handy Gumshoe Gangster Grabber," Albert bragged.

Ashley and I grinned at each other. Another gadget that actually worked!

"Let's continue this discussion in the library," Fiona said.

Everyone followed Fiona into the house. Albert tugged Martin inside by his yo-yo string.

"You're barking up the wrong tree," Martin growled. His butler voice seemed to have disappeared. "What makes you think I would want that kitty collar?"

"Because there's more to you than meets the eye, Martin," I said.

"Same diamonds, same shifty eyes, even the same suit," Ashley said. "Admit it, Martin. You're related to Shifty-Eyes Malone."

Martin struggled under the yo-yo rope. Then he shook his head and sighed. "Okay, you got me," he said. "My real name isn't Martin—it's Moe Malone. Better known as Shifty-Eyes Malone III."

"Aha!" Albert cried. "A chip off the old block. The old cell block, that is."

"Shifty was my grandfather," Moe explained. "He gave me the stickpin when I was a kid. I had the diamonds set into that ring." He nodded toward the ring in Ashley's hand.

"But that's not all I got from him," Moe continued. He stuck out his chin. "I also got his talent for stealing jewels."

"And all this time I thought you were my butler." Fiona sighed.

"I only pretended to be a butler so I could work in this house," Moe explained. "I wanted that collar!"

Just then, a police siren sounded outside the house.

"How did the police find out so quickly?" I asked.

"I called them," Albert said. He pointed to his walkie-talkie sneakers. "These things get more than just baseball games, you know."

We watched as the police came inside to lead Moe away.

"Imagine," Fiona said. "He had the nerve to put my poor puffy, fluffy angel inside that stuffy vase."

"Look, lady," Moe called over his shoulder. "I may have lifted the collar. But I didn't hide the cat."

He nodded at Patty. "*She's* the one who

did it," he said, sneering. "I saw her stuff the cat inside the vase with my own eyes."

"Patricia!" Fiona gasped. "Is this true?"

All eyes were on Patty as the police put Moe in the car and drove away.

"It's true, Great-grandmother," Patty whispered. Her eyes filled with tears. "I just wanted you to spend some more time with me. The way you used to before you got Flapper."

Fiona's eyes opened wide. "Oh, dear," she said. "I had no idea you felt this way."

Patty wiped away a tear. "I'm so sorry."

"No, I'm the one who's sorry," Fiona said with a smile. "And I'm going to make it up to you. We'll have lunch on Monday, go to the ballet on Tuesday, and then do some shopping on Wednesday. How does that sound?"

"Awesome," Patty said. She seemed totally cheered up. "And I won't even mind if Flapper comes, too."

I grinned at Ashley. This looked like the start of a beautiful friendship.

"Now let's get back to the ballroom," Fiona announced. "So the real dance contest can begin!"

"Poor Martin," Ashley shook her head. "He danced his heart out for nothing."

"Well we couldn't tell him we were setting him up," I pointed out.

"That's true," Ashley said. "And thanks for letting us break our promise, Patty, so we could tell Fiona about our plan."

"Anything to catch the thief," Patty replied.

"You two really are good detectives," Albert told Ashley and me as we all left the library. "Even without gadgets."

"They're not just good," Patty said. "They're the cat's meow!"

Hi from both of us,

Olsen and Olsen ahoy! Ashley and I went off on a fantastic Caribbean cruise with our family. The ship was amazing. The whole crew dressed like pirates. The captain had a sneaky pet monkey. There was even a talking parrot on board!

But the best part of the cruise was a kids' super scavenger hunt. Ashley and I were on our way to winning—until someone started stealing the prizes! It was up to us to find out who. Could we sail to the bottom of this case—before all the fun took a dive?

Want to find out more? Turn the page for a sneak peek at our next mystery, *The Case of the High Seas Secret.*

See you next time!

Mary-Kate Olsen   *Ashley Olsen*

A sneak peek at our next mystery…

The Case Of The
HIGH SEAS SECRET

"Look, there's Georgina!" I said.

The cruise director was leaving the staff room. She looked angry.

"Let's follow her," Ashley said. "Maybe she'll lead us to the missing prizes."

Ashley pulled out two baseball caps and two pairs of sunglasses from her backpack. "Here," she said. "Disguises."

We tailed Georgina all the way to the ship's dining room. Suddenly, we saw her duck behind a small palm tree. Then she took out a cell phone from her skirt and dialed.

Ashley and I tiptoed to a palm tree on the other side of the room. We peered out from between the large green leaves.

"I'm telling you, I can't take it anymore!"

Georgina was saying. "I'll do anything to get off this ship!"

Anything? Ashley and I looked at each other. Georgina sounded desperate, all right. Desperate enough to steal the prizes?

There was a sudden noise behind us. Georgina quit talking and flipped her phone closed. Then she hurried downstairs to the main deck.

Georgina turned into the movie theater. It was dark and filled with laughing kids.

"I can't see anything!" I whispered.

"You've got your sunglasses on," Ashley reminded me.

"Oh." I quickly pulled them off. "Right."

We saw Georgina walk out another exit. We hurried through the theater to follow her. But by the time we reached the exit, Georgina had disappeared.

We stopped to catch our breath. Now we were in a dark, narrow hall.

"I think we're lost," I said.

"No way," Ashley said. "Detectives find lost things. They don't *get* lost."

"True. But this ship has fourteen decks," I reminded her. "All the halls and stairs look the same. We could be anywhere."

Ashley pulled a map of the *Jolly Roger* from her backpack. "I bet we're right here," she said, pointing. "We turned left back at the arcade."

"Nope," I said. "We turned right. And then—OUCH!"

Ashley's nails were digging into my arm. She was staring straight ahead.

I followed Ashley's gaze. On the wall in front of us was a big black shadow. It had a crooked body, wavy arms, and stubby legs.

My heart thumped. Ashley was still clutching my arm.

The shadow didn't move. Slowly, I turned around. Something was hiding in the dimly lit stairwell.

And it was waiting for *us*!

Reading Checklist

andashley

single one!

❏ It's a Twin Thing
❏ How to Flunk
   Your First Date
❏ The Sleepover Secret
❏ One Twin Too Many
❏ To Snoop or Not to Snoop?
❏ My Sister the Supermodel
❏ Two's a Crowd
❏ Let's Party!
❏ Calling All Boys
❏ Winner Take All
❏ P. S. Wish You Were Here

❏ The Cool Club
❏ War of the Wardrobes
❏ Bye-Bye Boyfriend
❏ It's Snow Problem
❏ Likes Me, Likes Me Not

Super Specials:

❏ My Mary-Kate & Ashley Diary
❏ Our Story
❏ Passport to Paris Scrapbook
❏ Be My Valentine
❏ Wall Calendar 2001

**Available wherever books are sold,
or call 1-800-331-3761 to order.**

Jet to London
with Mary-Kate and Ashley!

All-new movie!

Own it on video today!

ADVERTISEMENT

MAKE YOUR OWN MOVIE MAGIC™
WITH THE
MARY-KATE AND ASHLEY
CELEBRITY PREMIERE FASHION DOLLS

AVAILABLE
MARCH 2001!

Go behind the scenes as
Mary-Kate gets ready...

...and Ashley sets
the scene.

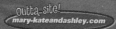

DUALSTAR
CONSUMER PRODUCTS

outta-site!
mary-kateandashley.com

mary-kateandashley

GAME GIRLS
mary-kateandashley
VIDEO GAMES

Join in on the Fun!

Real Games for Real Girls

Available NOW!